www.mascotbooks.com

For more information, please contact:
Mascot Books
620 Herndon Parkway #320
Herndon, VA 20170
info@mascotbooks.com

Library of Congress Control Number: 2018901570

CPSIA Code: PRT0318A
ISBN-13: 978-1-68401-613-6

Printed in the United States

Princess Ingeborg and the Dragons

Wendy Zomparelli

illustrated by Andrea Strongwater

ong ago, in a lovely little castle in a lovely little kingdom, there lived a princess. Her name was Matilda Angelina Elizabeth Rosemary Helena the Second, but everyone called her Ingeborg, for short.

Princess Ingeborg was not beautiful—few princesses are—but she had honest brown eyes, a kind smile, and a pleasant way of speaking that made you forget she was royalty. She lived in the castle with her father and mother (the king and queen, of course) and with her three older brothers.

The brothers were big and loud and brawny. They loved to hunt, to ride horses, and to hit things—mainly one another—with their fists and the flat sides of their swords.

Ingeborg's brothers spent most of their time questing. At first Ingeborg thought they were seeking the Holy Grail, but it turned out that they were looking for the Wholly Ale, a legendary beer. They would ride to taverns throughout the land, sampling every brew in hopes of discovering it, but they never did. Ingeborg thought her brothers were rather silly.

Her mother and father were intelligent, able rulers and very, very busy. Her father was constantly in meetings with councilors and ambassadors, and her mother managed the kingdom's finances and charities. They both received dozens of dispatches and letters every day and spent hours answering them.

In addition, all the regional royalty were caught up in a new craze called "chirping." They sent "chirps" of fourteen words or less on tiny parchment scrolls, writing things like, "Cook roasted a boar tonight and served it with buttered rutabagas—yum!" The scrolls were tied to the legs of trained robins, who would fly to the addressees' windows and chirp to announce their arrival, which was where "chirping" got its name.

To Ingeborg, it seemed that her parents always were reading or answering chirps or in meetings behind closed doors with guards in front. She often went days without seeing any of her family, and she sometimes felt lonesome. But she had dozens of books to read, and beautiful gardens in which to walk, and townspeople to talk to, and so she was content.

COOK ROASTED A BOAR TONIGHT AND SERVED IT WITH BUTTERED RUTABAGAS—YUM

not far from the castle, in a cavern overlooking a lush green valley and a shining blue lake, lived a dragon named Juno and her four children. The first dragon-child was named Esmeralda because of the streak of emeralds that ran from the top of her head to the tip of her pointed tail. The second was called Corona, which means crown, because of the orange and red flames that encircled her head whenever she spoke. The third, who was golden colored, was named Herbster, after his great-grandfather. And the fourth, the biggest of all the dragon-children, was named Bruce for no reason at all.

The dragon-children spent their days romping and playing. They were fond of floating on their backs in the lake, of hunting for tasty crawdads in the mud, and of playing hide-and-seek in the cave's dark passageways. Whenever it rained, the dragon-children would lie in the flowers and listen to the raindrops tinkling against their scales.

The dragons lived a happy, peaceful life, and they hardly ever left their valley. But beyond the valley there were towns and villages full of people who had heard of the dragons and feared them. And that was because of Sir Popenjoy.

Sir Popenjoy was an elderly knight with white hair and knees so knobby they rattled the armor on his legs. Once, while hunting, he had chanced upon the valley and had seen Juno playing with her children, who were just babies at the time.

"Ho, foul beast! I challenge thee to a combat!" Sir Popenjoy had shouted, charging his horse at Juno.

Juno knew there wasn't much the knight could do to hurt her, and she certainly didn't want to hurt him. So, when he got within range, she merely breathed out flames of medium heat—not hot enough to injure Sir Popenjoy, but hot enough to melt the tip of his spear.

The knight rode back to town as fast as he could. He told people that he had been ambushed by five huge dragons and had fought them off until his spear melted, forcing him to retreat.

Everyone believed Sir Popenjoy and told him what a great hero he was. So, the next time he told his story, he put another dragon in it to make himself sound braver. The more Sir Popenjoy told his story, the more dragons he added. Eventually, everyone believed the valley was filled with dozens of ferocious, snarling dragons. No one ever dared to go there.

One morning Juno said to her dragon-children, "My dears, you are 25 years old today, and it's time you had your first lessons in flying." (You may be surprised to learn that the dragon-children were 25, but remember that dragons live a very, very long time and are not considered to be adults until their 100th birthday.)

Flying! For years the children had dreamed of the day they would spread their bright wings and soar above the valley. Juno led them into the meadow where she taught them warm-up exercises, such as wing-flapping and claw-touching. Then she had them practice little takeoffs and landings by jumping off a large boulder. Finally, she took them to the top of the cavern and let them glide down into the lake. The dragon-children had never had so much fun.

Then Juno said, "Now I will take each of you on a flight, one at a time. You must promise to stay close to me and do whatever I tell you."

"We promise," they all said.

"Come, Esmeralda. You and I will go first," said Juno. And she took off with Esmeralda close beside her.

How glorious it is to glide over the hills, thought Esmeralda. *How warm the sun feels and how cool the breeze! How thrilling it will be to play tag in the clouds with Bruce, Corona, and Herbster!*

Juno and Esmeralda flew high over fields and villages, over dark forests and flowering orchards. Soon they came to a town, in the center of which stood a grand building with pennants fluttering from its towers.

"What is that, Mother?" asked Esmeralda. "It's beautiful!"

"That is the castle of the king and queen who govern this country," Juno answered. "Would you like a closer look?"

"Yes, please!" said Esmeralda.

They alighted on a roof overlooking the palace gardens. Esmeralda could see a strange creature sitting below them. It had a pale face and two arms, but in place of legs the creature had something long and blue.

"Mother, what is that?" she whispered.

"It is a human being, like the knight who came to our valley once," Juno replied. "But he was a male human, and this is a female human, just as Herbster and Bruce are male dragons, and you and Corona are females."

"Why doesn't it have any legs?" asked Esmeralda.

Juno chuckled. "It does, but they are underneath that blue covering, which I believe is called a dress."

"What is the dress for? Doesn't it get in the way of running? Why is the female human sitting alone like that?" Esmeralda asked.

"The ways of humans are generally so silly that we dragons do not waste much time thinking about them," Juno answered. "You would be better off thinking about your geography lessons, which you have been neglecting lately. Come, it is time to go home."

Weeks passed, and all the young dragons became accomplished flyers. Soon they had Juno's permission to fly wherever they wished, as long as they came home before supper and stayed out of trouble.

Esmeralda couldn't stop wondering about the female human being, sitting in the garden all alone. One morning she arose very early and flew to the palace to have another look at the fascinating creature. When Esmeralda landed in the garden, no one was there. She crawled into a stand of flowering azaleas and waited.

She didn't wait long. Soon the same female human (it was Ingeborg, of course) came walking across the grass. She sat on a bench under a tree, opened a book, and gave a deep sigh.

The dragon's heart was pounding. Would this creature speak to her? It was worth a try. "Hullo," said Esmeralda from the azaleas.

The female human being jumped up, calling out, "Who is there? What do you want?"

"I would like to talk to you, to find out who and what you are," replied Esmeralda.

When she saw a dragon crawling out from her azaleas, Ingeborg was too scared to move. She had heard terrifying tales of dragons carrying off maidens.

Esmeralda saw how frightened she was and stopped. "I won't hurt you," she said reassuringly, careful not to let any flames out of her mouth. "Really, I only want to talk. Besides, if I had come here to hurt you, I could easily have done so already."

Ingeborg saw the truth of this and relaxed. "Won't you sit down?" she asked.

"Yes, thank you," replied the dragon. She curled her long tail underneath her like a stool and sat on it.

"You must forgive me if I seemed rude," said the princess. "I have never seen a dragon before."

"And I had never seen a female human being before I saw you," said Esmeralda. "What is your name and what do you do?"

"My name is Matilda Angelina Elizabeth Rosemary Helena the Second, but everyone calls me Ingeborg. I am the princess here."

And what does a princess do?" inquired the dragon.

"Do? Well, not very much," said Ingeborg. "I read a lot and walk in this garden, and I take dancing lessons."

"Why do you cover your legs with that object?" asked Esmeralda. "I hope my questions are not impolite," she added.

"Oh, no," said the princess. "I like to have someone to talk to."

And she told Esmeralda about her dress and showed her the fine lace and embroidery that decorated it.

"But doesn't it get in the way when you run?" the dragon asked.

"Run? Princesses don't run!"

"Why not?" asked Esmeralda.

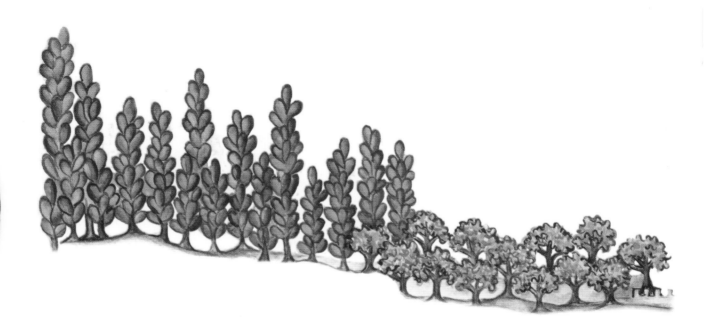

W hy not, indeed. Ingeborg was stumped. She couldn't say that she didn't want to run, because deep down she envied her brothers who were permitted to run all over the castle, laughing and shouting.

"I am not allowed to; I don't know why," she said at last. "But tell me who you are and what you do."

Esmeralda told the princess all about the valley, her mother, and how she played with her brothers and sister all day. She talked and talked, and Ingeborg listened eagerly to everything the dragon said.

"How wonderful your valley sounds," she said. "I must go back inside now, but please come and tell me more about it tomorrow."

Esmeralda promised to return, and then she took off for home.

Esmeralda flew back to the garden the next day, and the next day, and the day after that. Though Ingeborg did not complain, Esmeralda could tell that the princess was lonely. This made her sad. "I know," she said. "Why don't you come to the valley and visit my family? They will be happy to meet you, and we can play as much as we like. I will teach you how to run."

"Well, I don't know . . ." said Ingeborg.

"Do come," said Esmeralda. "I already asked my mother, and she said she would be honored to have you."

"Very well," the princess said. "But I must tell my parents." Ingeborg left Esmeralda waiting in the garden and went to her mother's chambers, but when she tried to enter a lady-in-waiting stopped her, saying that the queen was in an important conference and could not be disturbed. When she went to her father's reception room, the guard at the door said the king was meeting with his ambassadors and could not be interrupted.

Ingeborg went up to her room, and on her pillow she left this note:

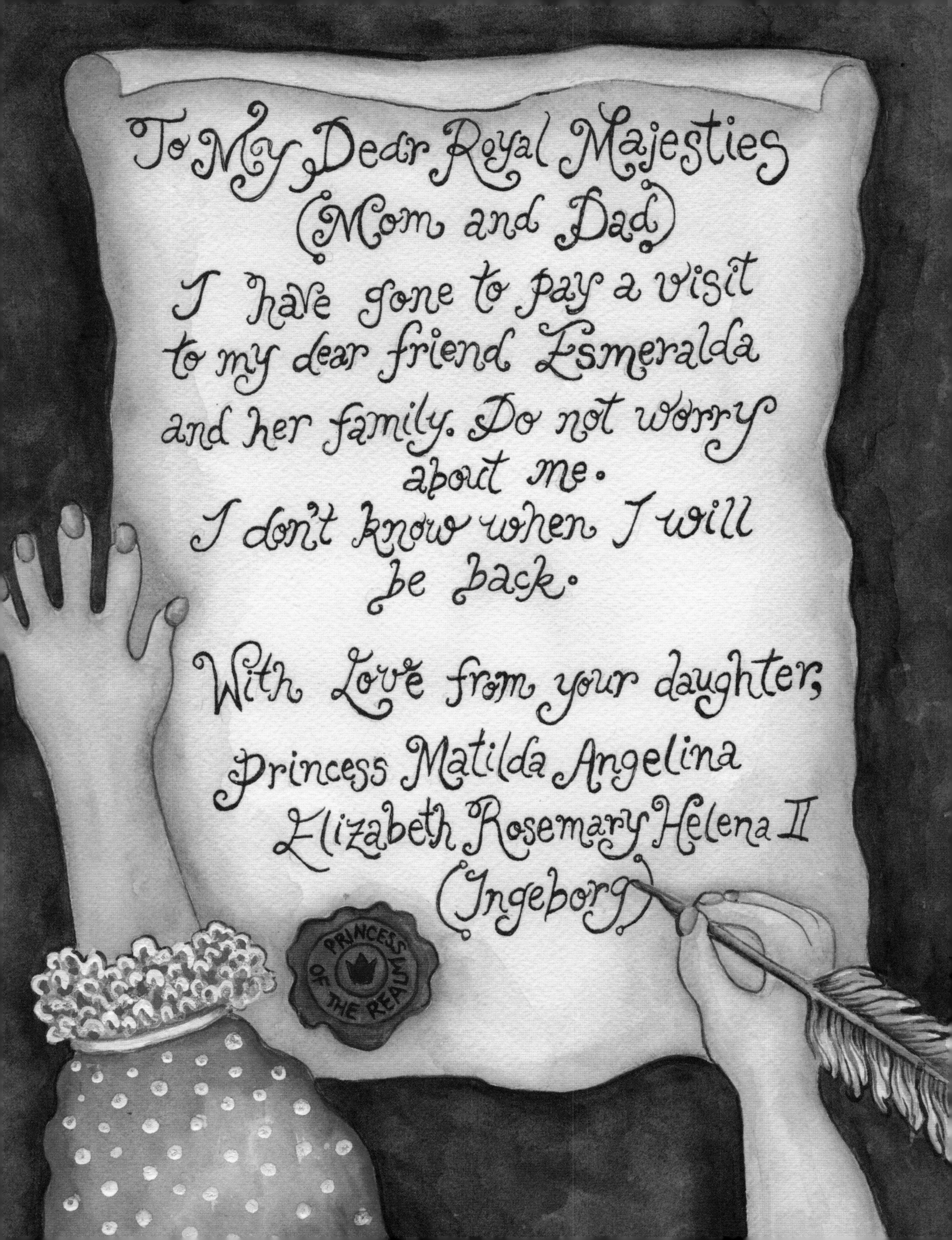

To My Dear Royal Majesties
(Mom and Dad)
I have gone to pay a visit
to my dear friend Esmeralda
and her family. Do not worry
about me.
I don't know when I will
be back.

With Love from your daughter,

Princess Matilda Angelina
Elizabeth Rosemary Helena II
(Ingeborg)

PRINCESS OF THE REALM

ngeborg packed up her toothbrush and a box of chocolate truffles and returned to the garden. She climbed up on Esmeralda's back and gasped with delight as the dragon leapt into the sky and sped away.

When they landed, the dragon family greeted Ingeborg enthusiastically. She presented the box of truffles to Juno who accepted them gratefully because (as everyone knows) dragons are very fond of chocolates. Then the dragons took Ingeborg on a tour of the valley. They climbed up the large rock that jutted over the lake, and Bruce demonstrated his favorite dive, a backwards flip with eight aerial somersaults.

"Oh," said the enraptured Ingeborg, "how I should love to dive into the lake!"

"Be our guest," said Juno.

"But I don't know how to swim," said Ingeborg.

"Don't know how to swim!" exclaimed Herbster, who was the best swimmer in the family. "It's easy! I'll teach you."

"But what will I wear to swim in?" asked Ingeborg. "This dress will be ruined if I get it wet."

"Let me see," said Juno. "We might have something you can use."

Everyone followed her up the trail to the dragon's cave. A short entrance tunnel opened into a large natural room with a high ceiling and with giant stalactites and stalagmites. This was where the family slept and ate and had lessons.

Off to the side was a smaller room with heaps of gold and jewels, swords and spears, and various bags and bundles.

"Where did you get all these things?" asked the amazed Ingeborg.

T his is our hoard," Juno explained. "It's like a lost-and-found. No self-respecting dragon can stand to see the countryside littered, so if we come across any trash, we bury it. But if we find something useful or pretty and we can't find its owner, we bring it home and store it here. Then, if the owner ever should come looking for it, we can return it."

They rummaged through the bags and bundles, looking for clothes for Ingeborg. Most of it was too big, but at last they found some shirts, trousers, and shoes that fit her—and a bright red bathing suit. Ingeborg quickly changed and ran laughing with her new friends down to the shore.

"Now then!" shouted Herbster. "Everyone into the water!"

All the dragon-children jumped into the lake with Ingeborg right behind. They taught her to hold her breath, kick her feet, and paddle with her arms. Soon she was cannonballing off the rock and playing water-tag.

That night, a very tired but happy princess lay down to sleep on a pile of sweet-smelling grass, with Esmeralda curled up beside her.

"Esmeralda," said the princess, "this has been the best day of my life."

The dragon yawned and smiled. "I'm glad," she said. "Sleep well."

And they did.

From that day, Ingeborg's life changed. She learned to run races and to hunt crawdads. She learned to climb trees and spent many happy hours chatting with Esmeralda in the treetops. Juno taught her how to speak the ancient Dragonish language and how to perform simple feats of magic, like disappearing.

As the weeks went by, the princess grew to love the dragons more and more. She loved their low-pitched voices, which had a slight hiss, and their shimmering scales of different colors. She loved their quiet politeness not only to her, but to each other, too. And if she happened to awaken in the middle of the night, she loved to watch the little red sparks that came out of the snoring dragons' mouths, lighting the cavern with a warm, rosy glow.

I have never felt so much at home in all my life, she thought, smiling.

One day, the king was strolling through the castle. *I haven't seen Ingeborg for quite some time,* he thought. *Perhaps I will stop by her room and see how she is.*

But when he got there the room was empty. He picked up the note from Ingeborg's pillow. *Esmeralda?* he said to himself. *I don't recall any royal families around here with a daughter named Esmeralda.*

The king interrupted the queen's meeting with the Society for the Improvement of Civic Improvements to ask if she knew of a Princess Esmeralda. The queen did not, so they sent chirps to all the neighboring kingdoms to ask if Ingeborg were there. All the replies said no.

The king and queen grew worried, so they ordered the soldiers to scour the countryside and find the princess. The troops searched for several days, but they found no trace of her.

Then the king remembered the stories of a valley full of dragons. He sent for Sir Popenjoy and asked him to journey to the dragon valley once again to see if Ingeborg was there. The king warned the knight not to fight the dragons or take any chances. "Just bring back a report," he said.

Off Sir Popenjoy rode. When he got to the edge of the valley, he crept cautiously up the rocky hillside and peered over. What he saw made him gasp.

There, sitting on the grass, surrounded by five large dragons, was the princess.

Sir Popenjoy rode back to the king as fast as he could. "Oh, sire!" he exclaimed. "The princess has been kidnapped by the dragons!"

The king summoned all the townspeople. "The horrible reptiles of the valley have captured my daughter!" he shouted to the crowd. "We must take up our weapons and march to that valley. The princess must be rescued! These pests must be exterminated! I call upon all loyal citizens to march with me today!"

Everyone cheered at these stirring words. The king, queen, and Ingeborg's brothers put on their armor, mounted their chargers, and marched off with Sir Popenjoy leading the way. Next came the archers and foot soldiers, then dozens of townspeople armed with sticks, frying pans, and pitchforks.

Of course, what Sir Popenjoy had seen was Ingeborg telling a story to the dragons, who sat in a circle to listen. Afterwards, Esmeralda and Ingeborg decided to fly to some nearby woods to look for berries. So when the royal family, troops, and townspeople rushed into the valley only Juno, Corona, Herbster, and Bruce were there. The king lunged so quickly at Juno that she barely had time to melt the end of his sword before it struck her metal scales.

"Quick, children!" Juno shouted. "Back to the cavern!"

The children ran while Juno used her flames to keep the attackers back. Then she, too, retreated and stood at the front of the cavern, facing the king, her children by her side.

"What is the meaning of this?" she called. "Be gone! We have done nothing to harm you."

"Nothing to harm me?" shouted the king. "You have captured my daughter, you snakes. Return her to me at once!"

"Your daughter came here of her own choosing, as our guest," Juno replied. "She is not here now, or she would tell you so herself."

"You lie, you fork-tongued monster! Attack, good people!" shouted the enraged king. The soldiers and townspeople rushed at the dragons, brandishing their swords, spears, sticks, and cookware.

"Do not hurt these people if you can avoid it, children," Juno said. "Keep them back with your flames and hope that Esmeralda and Ingeborg return soon."

As she added another blackberry to her basket, Ingeborg heard a distant clamor. "What can all that noise be?" she asked. "It sounds like a great crowd of people shouting."

Esmeralda raised her head and listened. "I think it is coming from our valley," she said. "Let's go see what it is."

Without another word they flew back to the valley. When she saw the outnumbered dragons defending themselves, Esmeralda put on a burst of speed. "We must save them!" she shouted. "We must fight!"

"No, wait!" said Ingeborg. "I have a better idea." She whispered some words into the dragon's ear. Esmeralda nodded and swooped down.

S TOP THIS FIGHTING!" Ingeborg shouted as they circled above the battle. "STOP IT AT ONCE! I, THE PRINCESS MATILDA ANGELINA ELIZABETH ROSEMARY HELENA THE SECOND, COMMAND YOU TO LAY DOWN YOUR WEAPONS!"

Everyone looked up, astonished to see the princess riding on a dragon's back, her long hair streaming out behind her. "Ingeborg! She is safe!" murmured the crowd.

Esmeralda landed in front of the cavern, between the dragons and her parents. "What is the meaning of this outrage? Why have you attacked my friends?" Ingeborg demanded.

"My dear, we came to rescue you from these monsters," the queen replied.

"Rescue me?" said the angry princess. "Didn't you get my note? I told you I was coming to visit Esmeralda's family."

"But you didn't say Esmeralda was a dragon," said the king. "You must come home right away. Princesses are not allowed to visit dragons. And where is your beautiful dress?"

"Beautiful dresses are all very well," Ingeborg replied, "but they get in the way of crawdad-hunting. Besides, I don't want to go home. There's not much for me to do at the castle. I would rather stay here."

The king and queen were alarmed. They knew that Ingeborg could climb up on Esmeralda's back and fly wherever she wanted, so they couldn't force her to return.

"But darling, the palace is where you belong," urged the queen. "You really ought to come home."

The princess told them how happy she had been with the dragons—how she had learned to swim and play and do a little magic, and how lonely she had been before meeting Esmeralda. "I know you both have very important jobs," she said, "but sometimes I would like to feel that I'm important to you, too."

*J*ust then, a weary robin landed on the king's shoulder, chirping faintly. The king untied the little parchment from its leg and read, "My jester just made a funny face while standing on his hands— JOL!!" (Which stood for Jolly Old Laugh.) He showed it to the queen, and they exchanged sheepish looks.

"I think, my dear, that we may be spending too much time on things that are not of the first importance," said the queen. "I could let other people chair some of my committees and reduce the time I spend in meetings."

"So can I!" the king agreed. "I shall let my ministers run our kingdom's routine business, and I shall attend only those meetings that are necessary to keep everyone safe, prosperous, and happy.

"And as for these silly parchments . . . " He turned to the robin. "Your services, and those of the other robin messengers, are no longer needed. As a token of our appreciation, you and your friends will always find cake crumbs on the palace windowsills." The delighted bird flew away.

The queen whispered briefly to the king, then turned to Juno. "It is my great pleasure to proclaim you and your family to be our kingdom's DFFs—Dragon Friends Forever," she announced. "Your portraits will be hung in our banqueting hall. You may visit Ingeborg at any time, and we look forward to becoming better acquainted with you."

The townspeople cheered. None of the other kingdoms had DFFs. And they couldn't get over how tall and strong Ingeborg had grown. As they walked back to their homes, they spoke of nothing else.

The princess hugged Juno, Corona, Herbster, and Bruce. "I will come to visit you often," she said.

"And you will always be welcome," Juno replied. "Our cave is your cave."

Then Ingeborg turned to Esmeralda. "Without you I wouldn't have learned that I can do and be much more than I ever would have thought. Won't you come live with me at the palace?"

Esmeralda couldn't bear to see her friend go. She gave big goodbye hugs to her mother and siblings, then off she flew with Ingeborg perched proudly on her back, waving to the people below.

many years passed. Ingeborg and Esmeralda spent most of their time in town, but they returned to the valley every summer to frolic in the sun with the dragon family.

For a long time, no one would believe anything Sir Popenjoy said because of the falsehoods he had told. To make up for causing so much trouble, the knight worked diligently on many civic improvement projects, cleaning rubbish out of the stream and planting geraniums in the square. Eventually he regained his neighbors' respect and was elected Fire Chief, an office he filled bravely and honestly for the rest of his life.

Ingeborg grew more accomplished every year, mastering all that her tutors could teach. She became one of the fastest runners in the kingdom, and no one could match her swimming—no one except Herbster. She had a kind word for everyone and was ready to help out in any way. Whenever the townspeople saw her strolling with Esmeralda they would say, "How lucky we are to have such a princess! And such a dragon!"

When the king and queen died, the oldest prince prepared to take the throne. But the people gathered at the castle and said, "We wish to be governed by the princess, who is the kindest, wisest person in the land."

The prince was delighted, because he didn't want to give up his quest for the Wholly Ale, and Ingeborg accepted the job. She ruled wisely and well, relying on the advice of her Chief Counselor and Minister for Dragon Affairs, Esmeralda.

The End

About the Author

The first thing Wendy remembers writing was her own newspaper, which featured an interview with the cartoon character Woody Woodpecker. She was 6 years old. She didn't know it then, but journalism was to become her career. She wrote for *The Raleigh Times, The News & Observer,* and *The Roanoke (Va.) Times.* In Roanoke, she eventually was named the editor and then the publisher.

Upon retiring, she moved from Roanoke to Charlottesville—and from non-fiction to fiction. She has written two novels and has plans for a third, as well as more adventures for Ingeborg and Esmeralda. When she isn't writing, she loves reading, gardening, cooking, and playing video games . . . but only games with elves and dragons in them.

About the Illustrator

Andrea has been an artist since the day she could hold a pencil and brush. Her first collected piece, saved by a friend's mother who saw something special, was a painting done in nursery school illustrating life for orphans in another country. Making art for others to enjoy and understand has always been Andrea's goal. For her, each piece needs to be beautiful and have a message, even when the message is as straightforward as, "This gorgeous blue makes me happy!"

Andrea was born in and lives in New York City and has also resided in Paris, France, and Old San Juan, Puerto Rico. Her work includes costumes and sets for theater and dance, clothing and textile development, writing and book illustration, decorative patterns for home products, jigsaw puzzles, greeting cards, mosaics, painting, and sculpture of all kinds. Her embroidery work has been used to create teaching programs in Afghanistan. Andrea makes beautiful things all day almost every day.

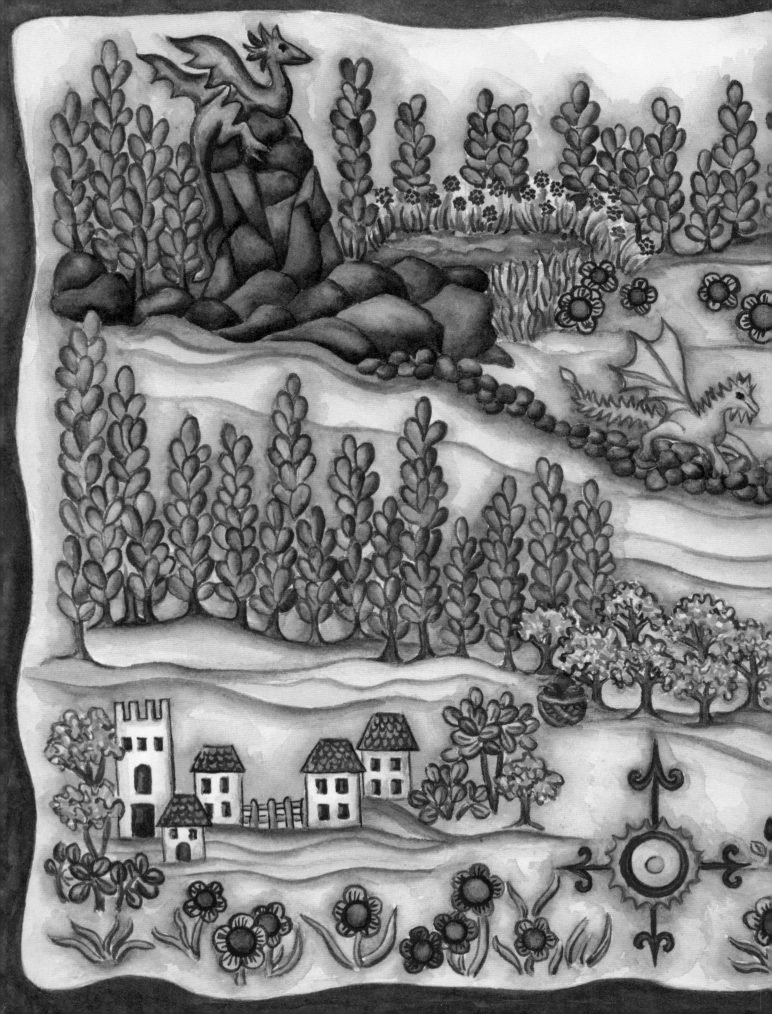